Dude, Where's My Spaceship?

For Judith and Zack. The truth is out there.
—D.G.

Dude, Where's My Spaceship?

by Dan Greenburg

illustrated by Macky Pamintuan

A STEPPING STONE BOOK™

Random House   New York

Copyright © 2006 by Dan Greenburg
Illustrations copyright © 2006 by Macky Pamintuan

Published in the United States by Random House Children's Books,
a division of Random House, Inc., New York.

RANDOM HOUSE and colophon are registered trademarks and
A STEPPING STONE BOOK and colophon are trademarks of
Random House, Inc.

www.steppingstonesbooks.com
www.randomhouse.com/kids

Educators and librarians, for a variety of teaching tools, visit us at
www.randomhouse.com/teachers

Library of Congress Cataloging-in-Publication Data
Greenburg, Dan.
Dude, where's my spaceship? / by Dan Greenburg ;
illustrated by Macky Pamintuan. — 1st ed.
p.   cm. — (Weird planet ; 1)
"A Stepping Stone Book."
SUMMARY: When their spaceship crash-lands on Earth, Ploo is captured by the
Army and taken to the mysterious Area 51, and while her brothers, Lek and
Klatu, try to rescue her, Ploo uses her ESP to make a new friend.
ISBN 0-375-83344-7 (pbk.) — ISBN 0-375-93344-1 (lib. bdg.)
[1. Extraterrestrial beings—Fiction. 2. Brothers and sisters—Fiction.
3. Extrasensory perception—Fiction. 4. Area 51 (Nev.)—Fiction.
5. Humorous stories. 6. Science fiction.] I. Pamintuan, Macky, ill. II. Title.
PZ7.G8278Dud 2006
[Fic]—dc22   2005027117

Printed in the United States of America
10 9 8 7 6 5 4 3 2 1
First Edition

Contents

Close Encounters of the Worst Kind

"EEEEEEEEEEEEEEEEEEEEEEEEEEEEEEE
EEEEEEEEEEEEEEE!"

The screams of three kids were the only
sounds in the small spacecraft. It fell out of
the sky, going way too fast. It was going so
fast, it glowed red.

This is not my fault, thought Klatu. He
was steering the spacecraft. *I did everything
the book said. Well, almost everything.*

The speed of the spacecraft's fall pulled at the skin on the kids' faces. The skin rippled.

Klatu's little sister, Ploo, looked at her reflection in the glass. *The rippling skin is interesting,* she thought. *Like waves in a pool. So that is what happens when you go too fast in a spacecraft.*

The smell of something burning began to fill the cabin.

The bad thing is, I am about to die, thought Lek, Klatu and Ploo's brother. *The good thing is, I will never have to do homework again.*

It was getting hot in the spacecraft. All three kids were sweating inside their foil space suits.

The spacecraft began to shake. Klatu, Ploo, and Lek felt the shaking in their bones and teeth.

I wonder what it will feel like to die, thought Ploo. *Probably not much fun, but at least it will be interesting. I wonder if the dead get to read a lot.* She used E.S.P. to send a thought message directly to her big brother's mind: Did you remember to turn on the anti-gravs, Klatu? she esped.

Of course I turned on the anti-gravs, Klatu esped back. I am not stupid, Ploo. When Ploo wasn't looking, Klatu reached over and turned on the anti-gravs.

The spacecraft slowed down. The skin on the kids' faces stopped rippling.

Maybe we are not going to die, thought Lek. *That is a good thing. The bad thing is, now I will have to keep doing homework. Which is worse? Hmm.*

Ploo looked out the window of the spacecraft. This planet was mostly desert. But way off in the dark distance lay a blanket of tiny, twinkling lights. A colony of clever aliens!

Ploo saw the planet rushing up to meet them. All the kids screamed.

The spacecraft landed very hard. It bounced and skidded toward a huge rock. Would it stop before smashing into the rock? The kids held their breath. The spacecraft dug a long trench in the sand before it shuddered to a stop. It missed the rock by inches.

Red and blue lights blinked on all over the ship. A loud warning buzzer buzzed.

"Everybody out!" Klatu shouted. "Fast! This thing could blow up!"

The three kids scrambled out of their seats. They squeezed out of the tiny, round exit door. One by one they plopped onto the cool sand. They rolled away from the spacecraft.

Ploo had a headache. Lek had a neck ache. Klatu had a nose ache. But they were all glad to be alive. What would happen to them now on this strange planet? What weird creatures would they meet?

Maybe these creatures will have long, horrible teeth, Lek worried. *If they have long, horrible teeth, will they chew me up? Or will they swallow me alive? Which would I hate more, being chewed up or being swallowed alive? Being swallowed alive would be less painful. But if I were chewed up, I would not feel the burning of the creature's stomach juices. Hmm.*

Ploo, Lek, and Klatu breathed in the cool night air. They'd heard they could breathe on this planet without oxygen tanks. They took a few steps in the sand. They had no trouble moving around. The gravity here was the same as back home. The only sound was the wind.

The stillness was broken by a faint puttering noise.

"Uh-oh," said Klatu. "Someone is coming. Hide!"

The three kids ducked behind a dune. The puttering noise grew louder.

"Klatu, they will see the spacecraft!" cried Ploo. "Do you have the hide-a-craft?"

"No, Ploo," said Klatu.

"Where is it, Klatu?" Ploo asked. "Quick!"

"I . . . might have left it inside," said Klatu.

This was awful. The spacecraft was their home away from home. If someone saw it, they'd want to take it. Then Lek, Klatu, and Ploo would be stuck on this planet forever!

Before anyone could stop her, Ploo darted out from behind the dune. She ran to the spacecraft and squeezed inside.

Lek and Klatu saw headlight beams. A

black truck bounced over the top of a dune. It was coming closer.

Ploo pulled herself out of the spacecraft. In her hand was a small remote control, the hide-a-craft. She pointed it at the spacecraft and clicked a button.

The spacecraft got blurry. And then it was gone!

The black truck stopped. It shone a bright spotlight on Ploo.

Two giants jumped out of the truck. They were the biggest creatures the kids had ever seen. They wore tan uniforms, black boots, and helmets.

Ploo dropped the hide-a-craft in the sand. She reached into the pocket of her space suit and pulled out a pack of language gum.

The taller giant ran over to Ploo. He snatched the language gum out of Ploo's hand. He grabbed her arm and pushed her toward the black truck. Her body was shaking with fear.

Lek! Klatu! What are these creatures? Ploo esped.

I think Earthlings call this place Nevada, esped Lek. They must be Nevadonians! No, NevaDOONians. Or is it NevaDOWNians? Hmm.

What do they want from me? esped Ploo.

They probably want to look you over, esped
Klatu. They have not seen many visitors from
our planet. Do not worry. We will rescue you!

When, Klatu? Ploo esped.

Soon, Ploo. Trust me. Have I ever let you down?

Lots of times, Ploo esped.

"Just look at that thing," said the taller

giant. He was from the top-secret Groom Lake army base, Area 51. He pointed at Ploo. "Is that alien ugly or what?"

"Ugliest thing I ever seen," said the shorter giant. "Look at its big head. And those huge eyes. And its disgusting gray skin. Ugh!"

"What was that thing reaching for?" asked the taller giant.

The shorter giant opened the pack of language gum balls and looked.

"Huh. Different-colored little balls, like marbles," he said. "Could be some kind of weapon. Lucky I got to it first, or we'd be in little bitty pieces now."

They pushed Ploo into their truck and took off for Area 51.

2

Playing with People's Minds

Ugly? Ugly? thought Ploo. She was very annoyed. *I am not ugly. Why did they say I am ugly? Lek tells me that I am beautiful. He says that I have pretty eyes. Even Klatu thinks I am pretty. These giant Earthlings are the ones who are ugly. Their skin is gross and pink. Their heads are too small. And their eyes are teeny-weeny. Yuck! Worse than Lightsiders.*

One side of Ploo's planet, Loogl, was

always dark because it faced away from its sun. Ploo and her brothers lived on the dark side of Loogl. Darksiders had huge eyes so they could see in the dark. Lightsiders had pink skin and beady little eyes like these Earthlings. Lightsiders and Darksiders didn't like each other much.

Ploo looked out the window. The road through the desert was rocky. The desert was spooky. She saw low sand dunes and spiky desert plants, lit by the full Earth moon. *They have only one moon, instead of six,* she thought. *How funny!*

Where were these creatures taking her? What would they do to her?

It had been a really dumb idea to come to Earth. But Klatu had just gotten his pilot's license, and he wanted to show that he could make a long trip. And Klatu said they could do extra-credit projects for school.

Klatu was a *varna,* but she still loved him. Ploo wondered how long it would take Klatu and Lek to find a way to rescue her.

The taller human put a white stick in his mouth and set it on fire.

From watching Earth TV, Ploo knew the sticks were called *cigarettes.* She decided humans sucked smoke into their bodies for warmth.

Ploo wondered if she could enter the thoughts of a human. She closed her eyes and tried to relax. She allowed her antenna, thin as a drinking straw, to slide quietly out of her head. She tried to enter the mind of the human who wasn't driving.

The human's mind was a very small space. There were nasty things inside it, coiled up tighter than fists. All of his thoughts were in black and white, not in lovely colors. . . .

The human was thinking: *I can't wait to show them the alien we captured. Yeah, that's right—captured. Captured after a nasty fight. Darned alien pulled out a ray gun and shot at us. It would've killed us, but the shot missed and hit a boulder. It shattered the darned boulder into a million little bitty pieces. I dove and tackled the creature. It grossed me out to even touch it, but I threw it to the ground. Saved our butts. . . .*

Hmm. This Earthling couldn't even tell the truth to himself.

What could she do with the thoughts of this silly human? Her mind gently grasped the human's mind like a lump of clay. She squeezed a little here, pinched a little there. What was the human thinking now?

. . . I wish we were back at the base already, he was thinking. *I can't wait to show them what we caught. A beautiful little alien girl. With gorgeous black eyes and velvety-soft gray skin. I'm ashamed to admit it, but I was so scared of her, I almost peed in my pants. . . .*

She liked his thoughts better now, much better. Maybe she could work with him. She trickled another thought into the human's mind: Let the beautiful little alien girl go. Nobody knows there is an alien. She is so beautiful, and she never hurt you. Stop the truck and let her go. . . .

Okay, I'll let the little alien girl go, the human was thinking. *No! Wait! General Stinkfellow's orders are: Bring all aliens back to the base. We can't disobey the general's orders. . . .*

General Stinkfellow is a <u>varna</u>, Ploo esped. She wondered if humans had a word like **varna**. We do not have to follow the orders of a <u>varna</u> like General Stinkfellow. Stop the truck and let the beautiful little alien girl go. . . .

"No!" shouted the human. "Don't stop the truck!"

"What, Frank?" said the driver. He looked startled.

"Nothing," said the one named Frank. He blushed.

Ploo tried again: Stop the truck. Stop it now. Let the beautiful little alien girl go. . . . She could feel his mind shut down. She heard him groan.

"Hey, Frank, you all right?" asked the driver.

"Yeah, I'm fine," said Frank. "No, Phil, actually, I'm *not* fine. Actually, I'm feeling kinda sick. Must've had a bad cheeseburger at dinner."

"Whatever," said Phil.

I cannot do any more with this human's mind, thought Ploo. *Maybe I can do better with others.* She drew her antenna back into her head. *I wonder what will happen to me now.*

The English Gum

Lek and Klatu followed the black truck's tire tracks in the sand. Klatu was sick with guilt.

"Why did I drag Ploo halfway across the universe to this stupid planet?" said Klatu. "If I had not, she would be safe at home now. Safe at home, doing stupid little-girl things. Instead, she is being taken to some stupid Earthling army base."

"How do you know this?" Lek asked.

"I picked it up from their thoughts," said Klatu.

"Will they hurt Ploo?" Lek asked.

"I hope not," said Klatu. "But you better believe they are going to give her all kinds of tests. Just like we do when we capture humans."

"Where do you think they took her?" Lek asked.

"I picked up a name from one of their minds," said Klatu. "Groom Lake."

"I read about Groom Lake in history class," said Lek. "It is a top-secret base in Nevada. Area 51. It is where they sent the Great Ones."

"The Great Ones!" Klatu repeated.

At the mention of the Great Ones, Lek and Klatu broke into the well-known Looglish cheer for the four who'd crashed at Roswell, New Mexico, in 1947:

"Threes and twos and ones and zeros!
Name our bravest Looglish heroes!
Darkside, Lightside, all agree
Who'll go down in history:
Org and Murkel, Shemp and Kurth
Found semi-intelligent life on Earth!
Sis boom bam! Sis boom zest!
Great Ones, Great Ones, you're the best!"

"I did not think the Great Ones were sent to Area 51," said Klatu. "I thought they were sent to . . . Lek, what is the name of that state? Ohoho?"

"Ohio," Lek corrected. "You would know that if you had not failed Earth Geography."

"Ohoho, right," said Klatu. "Who needs to know Earth geography anyway?"

"Only aliens who crash-land on Earth. And whose sister gets kidnapped," said

Lek. "In which case, knowing something about the planet might be handy."

Klatu ignored him. They walked on.

Ahead of them was a cactus.

"Look, Lek," said Klatu. "A non-human life-form. Hello there, nonhuman life-form." The cactus didn't answer. "I said *hello*," Klatu repeated. He touched the cactus.

"Yowtch!" he shouted. "It bit me!"

"You must have scared it," said Lek.

There was a faint chugging sound behind them. It was another truck.

"Uh-oh, more humans are coming, Klatu," said Lek. "We had better hide."

"Or maybe we can get a ride," Klatu said.

"Are you *yonko*?" said Lek. "What if they are bad guys like the ones who took Ploo?"

"If they are bad, we will run away," said Klatu. "If not, we will get a ride."

"No human would pick up four-foot-tall aliens with big heads and huge eyes," said Lek.

"No," said Klatu. "But what if we morph into human shape? What if we chew English gum? Then who will know we are not from Nedava?"

"Ne-*va*-da," Lek corrected.

"That is what I said, Ne-*da*-va. We better try to get a ride, Lek. We have to get to that base fast and rescue Ploo. Do you have the language gum?"

"Here." Lek handed Klatu a gum ball. Then he gave him three more for good luck. Klatu popped one into his mouth.

"All right, time to morph," said Klatu. "Ready, little brother?"

"Ready, Klatu."

With a soft sound, the two boys grew upward and outward. Their arms and legs got thicker. Their heads got smaller. Their eyes shrank down to the beady little things that humans had.

Both boys had chosen haircuts and clothes they'd seen in their Earth textbooks. But their textbooks were old. *Very* old. They'd picked old-fashioned sailor suits

with short pants. Button shoes. Straw hats with ribbons. Lek turned his hat around three times for good luck.

Klatu checked Lek out. "Looking good," he said.

"Our new bodies won't last more than an *arp*," said Lek. "We have to find Ploo fast!"

They set the *arp*-timers on their arms. One *arp* of Loogl time was close to one hour of Earth time. There were fifty *mynts* in one *arp*. In fifty *mynts* they'd look like aliens again.

The change was barely done when a blue pickup truck came over the nearest dune.

The boys didn't know how to make the truck come to a stop. Klatu waved his leg. The truck stopped.

"Howdy, boys," said the rancher in the truck. He had shaggy black hair and a cowboy hat that was rolled up at the corners.

"Bonsoir, monsieur," Klatu greeted the man.

"Huh?" said the rancher.

Klatu, you *varna*, that is <u>French</u>, Lek esped.

Ooops, Klatu esped. Right. The blue ones are French. He spit out the blue gum. He popped another gum ball, a red one, into his mouth.

"Buenas noches, señor," said Klatu out loud.

Klatu, the red ones are <u>Spanish</u>! Lek esped.

"You boys aren't from around here, are you?" said the rancher.

Quickly Lek chewed up the green gum ball, the English one. "Actually, no," said Lek. "We are from . . . Ohio."

"No kidding?" said the rancher. "I got family back in Ohio. What town?"

"What town?" Lek repeated. He tried to think back to Earth Geography. "Cincinnati?"

"You're kidding me!" said the rancher. "My brothers live in Cincinnati. What part of Cincinnati?"

Lek, you <u>varna</u>, why did you say Cincinnati? Why did you not say Cleverland? Klatu esped.

"I mean," said Lek, "we were from Cincinnati to *begin* with. But then we came, uh, west." He tried to remember the map of the United States. West was right. Phew!

"Are you going to Groom Lake?" asked Klatu. "We could use a ride."

"Hop in," said the rancher.

Lek and Klatu hopped to the other side of the truck. They waited for the door to slide up into the roof of the truck. That was how doors worked on planet Loogl. But the door stayed shut.

"What's the matter?" the rancher asked.

"I think this door is . . . broken," said Lek.

"Broken?" said the rancher. "Heck, no. Look."

He reached across the seat and opened the door.

"Hmm," said Lek.

Lek and Klatu hopped into the truck. The rancher moved a stick attached to the floor. The truck growled and moved forward.

"Are you boys going to the army base?" asked the rancher.

"Yes," said Klatu.

No, you fool! Lek esped.

"No, you fool!" Klatu repeated without thinking.

"What?" said the rancher.

"Uh, I did not finish," said Klatu quickly. "No, you fool around near that base and they will arrest you."

Lek breathed a sigh of relief.

"You're sure right about that," said the rancher. "They got a lot to hide out there."

"What do they hide?" asked Lek.

The rancher lowered his voice. Lek and Klatu leaned in to hear him.

"UFOs," whispered the rancher. "And little green men from that flying saucer crash in Roswell."

"Why do you think they were green?" Lek asked.

"They were definitely green," said the rancher. "I know that for a fact."

"How do you know that?" Lek asked him.

Let it go, Lek! Klatu esped. *Why not let him think they were green?*

Because it is not the <u>truth</u>, Lek esped.

Who cares if it is the truth or not?

I do, Lek esped. *Truth is important to me.*

"How do you know the aliens were green?" Lek asked. "I heard they had *gray* skin."

"Gray? Well, you heard wrong," said the rancher. "It was green. I know a guy who *saw* one of them little buggers."

"Really?" said Lek. "Well, I—"

Klatu clapped his hand over Lek's mouth.

"Wow, green aliens," said Klatu. "Amazing!"

"Mmmff mmmff," said Lek.

A few minutes later, the rancher dropped them off in Groom Lake and waved goodbye.

The town of Groom Lake was hardly a town at all. There was a gas station and a grocery store. There was a diner and a bar with a neon sign. There was a little store that said ALDO'S PIZZA on the window. That was it.

About a mile off, Lek could make out the lights of the army base and the black shape of a mountain behind it. Far away, thunder rumbled.

A human walked his dog along the street. The dog pulled hard on its leash, dragging the human along behind it. The dog stopped to sniff something. The dog squatted and pooped. The human picked up the poop and put it in a little plastic bag.

Lek, did you see that dog? Klatu esped. Humans must be ruled by master dogs. They pull humans along on ropes. They make humans pick up their poop!

Dogs must be smarter than humans, esped Lek. Maybe they can help us.

Lek and Klatu caught up with the dog. Klatu esped it: Hello there, Mister Dog! We are from the planet Loogl. Our sister has been taken

to Area 51. We see that you dogs control the humans. Can you help us rescue her?

There was no answer from the dog. The dog didn't even look at Lek and Klatu. It just kept on walking and sniffing and pooping.

I do not think it heard you, Lek esped. *Let us listen to its thoughts.*

The dog was thinking, *Gotta smell <u>that</u>, gotta smell <u>that</u>! Whooh! I know exactly where that came from. Whoa, what's <u>that</u>? Gotta smell <u>that</u>! Gotta smell <u>that</u>!*

Okay, esped Klatu. *Maybe this is not one of the smarter dogs. We will ask another.*

Thunder rumbled again. Lek looked at his *arp*-timer. "Forty-five *mynts*, Klatu," he said. "Wait. Hmm. Actually forty-four. Only forty-four *mynts* left to rescue Ploo while we still look human."

"How are we going to get into the army base, smart guy?" asked Klatu.

Just then a boy came out of Aldo's Pizza, carrying a stack of flat cardboard boxes. He went to a station wagon at the curb and put them inside. Then he walked back into Aldo's Pizza.

"What are those flat boxy things?" Lek asked.

Klatu didn't know. But not knowing never stopped Klatu from answering.

"Turtles," said Klatu. "Box turtles."

"What are box turtles?" Lek asked.

"Flat boxy things that people put in cars," said Klatu.

Klatu walked over to the car. A wonderful smell was reaching his nose-holes. Klatu reached in through an open window. He took the top box off the stack and took a bite out of the box. The bite he took had no pizza in it, just cardboard.

"Mmm, this box turtle is delicious!" said Klatu. He took another bite out of the box. "If we took these box turtles to the base where they are holding Ploo, maybe they would let us inside," said Klatu.

"How would we get them there?" asked Lek.

Klatu looked at the car. He looked at the lights of the base in the distance. Lek saw the look and knew what Klatu was thinking. He shook his head.

"We cannot steal this car, Klatu," he said. "Stealing is wrong."

"It is not stealing, Lek. It is *borrowing*. After we rescue Ploo, we will give it back. We can even leave a few Looglish platinum coins on the seat. It is the only way to save Ploo."

Lek looked at his *arp*-timer. There were now just forty *mynts* left to look human.

Lek sighed. "Hmm." He wound his *arp*-timer three times for good luck. "Okay, Klatu. We will do it for Ploo. Can you figure out how to drive this car?"

Klatu put his arm around Lek's

shoulders. "Little brother, there is no vehicle in the universe that Klatu the Magnificent cannot drive," said Klatu. "Trust me."

Lek crept over to the station wagon. He reached in through the open window and opened the door. They crawled inside. Klatu pressed every button on the dashboard. He turned every knob. Nothing happened.

"I thought you said there is no vehicle in the universe that Klatu the Magnificent cannot drive," said Lek.

"Shut up, Lek."

Klatu turned a key. The motor started with a roar.

"Good job, Klatu! Now get us out of here!"

"I am working on it, little brother," said Klatu. He had no idea how to make the car move.

The boy from Aldo's Pizza came outside. "Hey!" he shouted.

"Now would be a great time to go, Klatu."

"I said I am *working* on it, Lek!"

Klatu still hadn't figured out how to make the car go. He remembered seeing the rancher move a stick in the floor.

The kid was running across the parking lot. He was still shouting.

Klatu moved the stick. He stomped on a pedal. The station wagon jolted backward. It hit the car behind it with a crunch. Then Klatu hit the horn button by accident. The horn stuck.

People ran out of the stores. They started shouting.

Klatu moved the stick the other way. He stomped on the pedal. The station wagon jumped forward. It hit a big trash can, but it bounced off and kept going.

"Klatu, you did it!"

"What did I tell you, kid?" said Klatu. "There is no vehicle in the universe that Klatu the Magnificent cannot drive!"

About twenty people were chasing after the station wagon now. But Klatu left them in the Groom Lake dust.

Lek looked at his *arp*-timer. Only thirty *mynts* left till their human forms slid back into the shapes of aliens. Less time than that till the English gum lost its flavor.

Where was Ploo? What were the humans doing to her? Would they be in time to save her? Lek was terribly worried.

Open Wide and Say "Aaaarrrggh!"

Ploo was in a cage that stood against the back wall of a huge lab. It was covered by a big black blanket. Ploo was listening to what the voices outside her cage were saying.

"Major Paine," said one voice, "newspaper and TV reporters keep calling about tonight's UFO crash. What should I tell them?"

"It wasn't a UFO, Sergeant," said another voice. "It was a weather balloon."

"Sir," said the first voice, "the reporters say aliens were seen fleeing the UFO. They know one of them was captured and is here at the base."

"Tell them there were no aliens, Sergeant," said the second voice. "Say there were crash dummies."

"Sir, what would crash dummies be doing in a weather balloon?"

"*I* don't know, Sergeant. Make something up."

"Yes, sir. Thank you, sir."

Ploo heard footsteps leaving the lab. Other footsteps came toward her cage. The black cover was pulled aside.

"Eeeeeee!" Ploo screamed.

A huge face was staring in at her. It had gray hair on top. It had bushy gray hair between the nose and mouth. The face looked excited and angry and scared.

Why did it look scared?

"So, you little monster," said the Earthling, "we caught you before you could harm the good people of Earth!

Are other aliens coming? We'll capture them, too!"

This Earthling's voice was one of the voices she'd just listened to. It was Major Paine. But why was he so mad? And what did he mean about harming the good people of Earth?

Ploo wished she had her English gum. She could have told him not to be scared. She could have told him that she was just a little girl. But her gum was on a table outside the cage.

The door at the other end of the room opened, and a very small Earthling burst in. It had lots of yellow hair at the top of its face.

"Daddy!" called the little Earthling.

Major Paine turned to look at it. "Oh, hi, Lily," said Major Paine in a nicer voice. "It's after eight o'clock. Why are *you* up so late, kitten?"

He called the Earthling "kitten." *Kitten* was the word for a baby cat. It didn't *look* like a baby cat.

"Mommy said you caught an alien. I wanted to see it."

The little Earthling ran over to Major Paine.

"It's in the cage," said Major Paine. He turned back toward Ploo. "Don't get too close. It's dangerous."

The little Earthling tiptoed up to the cage and stared at Ploo.

"Daddy, it's so little. Littler than *me*. It's *cute*."

"Cute?" He snorted with laughter. "It's little, but it could be as mean as a rattlesnake. It could be an alien scout. It could be planning to take over Earth. We don't know a thing about it. I was just about to examine it."

Major Paine hung a doctor's stethoscope around his neck. He put on a pair of heavy gloves.

"Can I watch, Daddy?" asked the little Earthling.

"Okay," said Major Paine. "But step back, Lily. I don't want it to attack you when I open the cage."

The little human stepped back. Major Paine reached into the cage. He placed the stethoscope against Ploo's chest.

"Hmm," said Major Paine. "Human heartbeat is about seventy beats a minute. This alien's is *four hundred* beats a minute. . . . No, I was wrong. The alien's heartbeat is only *two* hundred beats a minute. But it has two hearts!"

He stuck a thermometer in Ploo's mouth. She ate it.

He closed the cage. "See what I mean,

Lily?" he said. "These aliens are nothing like us. They're *dangerous*. Now go home, honey. Ask Mommy to put you to bed."

"Good night, Daddy!" The little Earthling threw its arms around Major Paine. Then it ran loudly out of the lab.

Ploo liked the little Earthling. It said she was cute. Finally, an Earthling with good taste!

After a few more tests, Major Paine finally left. Ploo relaxed. The lab was dark now. She liked the dark. It reminded her of home. Ploo heard a lock click and a door creak open. She heard footsteps echo in the huge building. They were little steps. Not big Major Paine footsteps. It sounded like another kid. It was Lily!

Hi, Lily, said Ploo in Lily's head. I am glad you came back.

Oooh, this is creepy! Lily thought. *How did you get inside my head?*

I am not inside your head, said Ploo. I am in a cage. Can you come closer?

No way, Lily thought. *I'm getting out of here!*

Wait! said Ploo. Please, Lily, I really need your help.

"Are you the alien?" Lily asked out loud.

Yes, esped Ploo.

"My daddy said you're mean," said Lily. "My daddy said you could be an alien scout. Are you planning to take over Earth?"

No, I am just a little girl. My name is Ploo. My brothers and I came here from another planet. My older brother Klatu crashed our spaceship. He is a varna. Do you know what a varna is?

47

"Is a *varna* like a klutz?"

Klutz? Probably. Anyway, my brothers are trying to resche me. Can you help me? Can you unlock my cage? Please?

"What if you're fibbing to me?" Lily

asked Ploo. "What if you're not a little girl? What if you're a monster, and you just want to get out of your cage and eat me?"

You are bigger than me, esped Ploo. How could I eat you? Lily, I am telling you the truth.

"Cross your heart?" Lily asked.

Ploo wondered what that meant. *Yes, both of them,* she esped.

Lily thought this over. She decided to trust the alien.

"Okay, I'll help you escape," said Lily. "But I can't see. Let me find a light."

No! No lights! They will come to find out why lights are on. I can see in the dark. Come here. I will guide you.

With Ploo's voice in her head, Lily walked across the floor of the lab. She reached the cage.

"I'll unlock the cage door," said Lily. "I have a key, but I don't know where the lock is. I can't see it in the dark."

Reach out your hand, Lily. I will move it to the lock, Ploo esped.

Lily reached out her hand in the darkness. Three very long fingers grasped Lily's hand. They were smooth, slippery, and cold. The touch of Ploo's hand made her shiver. It felt a little like a snake.

"Your hand is so . . . cold," said Lily.

Your hand is hot. Humans must be warm-blooded.

"Yes," Lily whispered.

Here is the lock. Go ahead and undo it.

"Okay."

Lily unlocked the lock. Ploo opened the cage.

Good. Now let us get out of here before somebody comes!

5

We've Got Seven Pepperoni Pies. Is Our Sister in There?

All the way to Area 51, Lek and Klatu boasted about how they would get through the entrance. But when they actually drove up to it, they no longer felt so brave.

There was a wooden gate across the entrance. It had zebra stripes in black and yellow. On top of the walls were rolls of barbed wire. Searchlights on the walls shone down at them. Big signs read: YOU ARE IN A TOP-SECRET AREA. GO AWAY! WHY DID YOU EVEN COME HERE?

This does not look good, Klatu, esped Lek.

A guard in a tan uniform came up to them. "This is a top-secret area," said the guard. "You can't be here."

Klatu looked at the guard and tried to speak. There was very little flavor left in his English gum, so it was hard.

"Hallo, mister. We are so pleased to . . . meeting you," said Klatu.

"What?" said the guard.

"We are . . . pleasing to . . . meet you," said Klatu.

It is not working! esped Lek. *Show him the box turtles!*

Klatu held out the pizza boxes. He closed his eyes. He waited for something to happen.

The guard moaned. "Mmm," he said. "That smells good."

It is working! esped Lek. He blew his nose three times for good luck.

"Who ordered this pizza?" asked the guard.

Why is he calling the box turtles pizza? esped Klatu.

Lek shrugged. Maybe he is trying to trick us.

"Soldier guy who . . . wear uniform with many buttons," said Klatu. "He order these box turtles."

"What is his name?" asked the guard.

"Remembering name is . . ." Klatu shook his head. "Remembering name is . . . major pain."

"Major Paine?" said the guard. "Very good. Park your car at the side of the gate and take them right in. Major Paine is in that large building right over there." He pointed. "The one where they keep the aliens."

The black-and-yellow-striped gate went up. The guard stepped aside.

What just happened? esped Klatu as he drove forward.

I do not know, esped Lek. *But did you hear him mention they are holding aliens? That must be Ploo! Let us get in there before he changes his mind.*

Carrying the stack of pizzas, Lek and Klatu hurried to the building the guard had pointed to.

Ploo! Ploo! esped Lek. He couldn't wait to see his sister again.

The building was locked. They broke a window and climbed inside. The building was empty. The cages along the back wall were empty, too! What had they done with Ploo?

6

Alien Girls Just Wanna Have Fun

Once they left the lab, Lily took the lead. She guided Ploo to an open field with tall grasses. A hedge hid them from the road that ran down the middle of the army base.

See? said Ploo in Lily's head. *I did not eat you. I was telling the truth.*

"You're my very first alien," said Lily. "I can't believe I know a real, live alien."

You are my fourth human, **esped Ploo.** I like you much better than the other three. Thanks for saving me! Where are we going?

"To my house."

To the house of Major Paine? **esped Ploo.** Is that a good idea?

"It's the only place I can think of," said Lily. "Uh-oh!"

A black truck came around a corner.

"Quick, Ploo! Get down!"

Both Ploo and Lily dropped to the ground. Somebody in the truck shone a searchlight toward where the girls were. They didn't move. The searchlight went out and the truck drove on. Lily helped Ploo get up.

They ran through the field and around the back of another building. They ran past the backyards of several houses. All the houses looked exactly alike. Small tan houses with tan roofs. Lily stopped at one of them.

"This is my house," Lily whispered. "This is my bedroom window."

The window was partly open. Standing on tiptoe, Lily pushed it higher. She pulled herself through it. Then she reached down to Ploo.

"Grab my hands, Ploo," she whispered.

Long alien fingers grabbed her hands. Lily pulled. Ploo was amazingly light.

Is this where you live? asked Ploo. She looked around the dark bedroom.

"Yes," said Lily. "Do you have your own room?"

Yes, but it does not look like this, esped Ploo.

They sat down on Lily's bed. It had a rainbow-colored bedspread. It had big, puffy pillows. There were about twenty dolls sitting against the pillows. Ploo looked at the dolls.

Why do you have so many baby humans? asked Ploo.

"They're not baby humans," said Lily. "They're not alive, they're dolls. Toys to play with. Where are you from, Ploo? Mars?"

Mars? Oh, you mean Gromple. No, esped Ploo. I am from the planet Loogl. My brother Klatu crashed our spacecraft. We have to get it fixed.

"Do you know how to fix it?"

Klatu pretends to know, esped Ploo, but he does not.

Lily giggled. "I have an older brother named Randy," she said. "He pretends to know a lot about cars. A whole lot. He doesn't. He's a . . . a *varna*."

Ploo giggled, too. Then they both started giggling together and couldn't stop. They giggled till they ached. They giggled till they could hardly breathe.

I don't have anyone to giggle with like this at home, said Ploo.

"Me either," said Lily. "Boy, I wish you didn't have to leave."

Me too, said Ploo. But we have to go back to our own planet. Our mother gets mad if we are

late for <u>snargle-ploom</u>. I wish there was somebody
who knew how to fix our spacecraft.

"I know a really nice lady named Jo-Jo,"
said Lily. "She can fix anything. She got one
of the UFOs that crashed here to fly again.
She used to babysit me."

When you were a baby, she sat on you? said
Ploo.

"No, no," said Lily. "*Babysit* means she took care of me when my mommy and daddy were working."

Can you ask Jo-Jo to fix our spacecraft?

"She's gone now," said Lily. "She didn't like taking orders, so they fired her."

They burnt her? said Ploo. How awful!

Lily laughed. "No, *fired* means they made her leave her job. She went to Las Vegas. I think she works in one of the big hotels there. . . . Uh-oh. Did you hear that?"

Someone is coming! said Ploo.

"Quick, Ploo! Hide!"

Will the Real Aliens Please Stand Up?

It has started, esped Lek. *I am melting, melting!*

Me too, esped Klatu. *Oh, I hate this part!*

Lek and Klatu had ducked behind a building when they began to morph. Their heads and eyes grew bigger. Their skin turned from pink to Looglish gray. The act of changing back made them very tired.

The stack of pizzas felt too heavy to carry. They dropped the boxes on the ground and flopped down beside them.

They were hungry, and the pizzas smelled delicious.

Klatu took a bite out of one of the boxes. This time his bite had pizza in it as well as cardboard.

"Rrrrrr," said Klatu. "This box turtle is even better than the one I ate before. There is something gooey and delicious in it."

Lek took a bite, too. "Rrrrrr, this is good. I hope gooey does not mean spoiled."

Lek and Klatu ate all the pizza, and all the boxes, too. It made them feel less tired.

"Now that we look like aliens again, how will we ever be able to save Ploo?" asked Klatu.

"I do not know," said Lek. "But maybe we are now in esping range." Hey, Ploo! he esped. It is Lek and Klatu! Are you there? Can you hear us?

There was no answer.

"It is no use," said Lek. "She cannot hear us."

Suddenly two humans in uniforms came around the corner of the building. It was the same two who had captured Ploo!

Run, Lek! Klatu esped.

Both boys turned around and ran away from the humans. But the humans had spotted them.

"After them, Frank!" yelled one.

"Right behind you, Phil!" yelled the other.

The two men took off after the alien boys.

Lek and Klatu ran along a hedge. They looked for somewhere to hide.

They ran past a row of shops. The signs read AREA 51 GROCERIES, AREA 51 DRUGSTORE, AREA 51 PET SUPPLIES. One read WEIRD PLANET GIFTS. In the window of Weird Planet Gifts was a big poster of a Loogling!

The two boys ducked inside the shop.

Everywhere they looked were posters, masks, and little plastic action figures. In the corner were blow-up dolls. All looked like *them*. Small, gray-skinned, big-headed dolls with huge black eyes.

"Hey, where did you get those cool costumes?" asked a voice behind them.

They spun around. The voice had come from—no. It was impossible! The voice came from a Loogling! Lek rubbed his eyes. Klatu's long mouth hung open. They looked closer.

No, it wasn't a Loogling. The gray skin was loose, wrinkled, and baggy. The big black eyes weren't deep and shiny, they were just flat black plastic. It was a human, a human dressed as a Loogling.

"Where did you get those cool costumes?" the human asked again.

Klatu looked at Lek. Lek looked at Klatu. They turned back to the human.

"Uh, we getting them . . ." Klatu's English gum had almost no flavor left. "We getting them from . . . *there*. . . ." Klatu waved his left arm.

"West? Do you mean California?"

asked the human. "Were you part of a movie? In Hollywood?"

"Yes, a movie . . . in Hollyhocks," said Klatu.

"Holly*wood*," Lek corrected him.

"That's fantastic!" said the human. "Your costumes are incredible. You look like real aliens. Well, until you get up close."

Frank and Phil burst into the gift shop. They spotted the shop worker in the alien costume and they stopped short. Frank looked confused.

"May I help you?" asked the worker in the alien costume.

It took Frank a second, but he figured it out. This was not a *real* alien.

"Uh, yeah," said Frank. "Did you see two aliens come in here a minute ago?"

"Sure," said the worker. "Their costumes were great." He turned around and looked behind him. "That's funny. They were standing here a second ago."

Phil and Frank ran through the shop. At the back of the store, they found them. The aliens' backs were to Phil and Frank.

"Stop!" yelled Frank. "Put your hands above your heads and turn around slowly!"

The two alien boys put their hands above their heads. They turned around slowly.

"What th—?" said Phil.

The two aliens had loose, baggy skin. Their big black eyes were flat plastic.

"It's just a couple of kids in cheesy costumes, Frank," said Phil.

Frank sighed loudly. "Oh, heck," he said. "Okay, you kids better get on home now, before your folks learn you're out late."

Or, thought Lek, *before you learn who we really are.*

8

Escape from Area 51

"Lily!" yelled her father. He stormed into his daughter's room. "Where is that darn alien?"

"What, Daddy?" said Lily. She yawned and stretched. She pretended she was just waking up.

"My men went to check on that alien," said Major Paine. "It's gone. Its cage is unlocked and my keys are missing. You wouldn't know anything about that, would you?"

"The alien is gone?" Lily repeated. "Golly!"

Major Paine went down on his knees. He shone a bright flashlight under her bed. He opened the big bottom drawer of her dresser and shone his flashlight inside. He yanked open the door of her closet and shone the flashlight in there, too.

He saw a big pile of laundry. Something was hiding under it, something alive.

"Well, well, well!" said Major Paine.

He began digging in the pile of laundry.

Out came . . . a springer spaniel puppy.

Major Paine shone his flashlight at the pup. He turned back to his daughter.

"Lily," said the major. "Where is the alien?"

"She followed me home," said Lily, pointing to the puppy. "Can I keep her, Daddy? Can I? Please?"

Major Paine sighed. He put away his flashlight. "We'll ask your mother in the morning," he said. "Right now I have to find that alien. I hope you had nothing to do with letting it go, or you'll be in big trouble, young lady." He left the room.

Lily got out of bed. She went into the closet and put her arms around the puppy.

"That was amazing, Ploo," she whispered. "How did you ever turn yourself into a puppy?"

We can change into other creatures for about an arp, Ploo esped. But it is tiring. I can hardly lift a paw now.

"Listen, Ploo," said Lily. "It's not safe here. My daddy could come back at any moment. We have to get you out of here. Follow me. Quick!"

Lily climbed through the window, carrying Ploo. Lily led the little alien around the back of her house. She led her down a dark alley and over a fence. A poodle in one of the yards barked at them. Ploo barked back.

Then a funny thing happened. A voice in Ploo's head said, Hello there, Mister Dog! We are from the planet Loogl. Can you help us find our sister?

Ploo turned around. She saw two figures coming toward her in the dark.

Lek? Klatu? esped Ploo. Is that you?

Ploo? We thought you were a dog!

I <u>am</u> a dog! esped Ploo. I thought I would never see you again!

Lek and Klatu hugged Ploo. They were still wearing their cheesy alien costumes.

Why is your skin so loose? Ploo asked.

This is not our skin, said Lek. These are costumes. Do not even ask. He pulled it off.

Lek, Klatu, this is Lily, esped Ploo. She is the wonderful little human who resched me.

"I am . . . pleasing to meeting you," said Lek out loud.

"I am the same . . . also as pleasing," said Klatu.

You can esp her directly, Ploo esped.

Thank you for saving our sister, esped Klatu.

If you ever need our help, just ask us, esped Lek. *We will do anything for you. Well, almost anything. I should probably mention a few things we will <u>not</u> do. . . .*

"Thanks," said Lily. "But we really have to get you out of here before my father comes looking for me. Come on!"

Lily led Lek, Klatu, and Ploo along a low line of bushes to another alley. They

went down the alley to the fence that ran around the whole base. Lily led them to a row of large trash cans. She moved the cans. Behind them was a small hole in the fence. It was big enough for a child, a dog, or an alien to crawl through.

"After you go through the hole, turn right," Lily whispered. "Follow the fence to the main gate."

Tell me again the name of the lady who can fix our spacecraft, Ploo esped.

"Her name is Jo-Jo," said Lily. "She works at one of the big hotels in Las Vegas. I don't know which one. Las Vegas isn't far from here, but it's too far to walk. Good luck!"

Ploo, Lek, and Klatu hugged Lily goodbye.

I will figure out some way to see you again, Lily, Ploo esped. *I promise.*

Lek, Klatu, and Ploo crawled through the hole and made their way toward the parked station wagon.

Ploo, who is this Jo-Jo you want to see in Las Vegas? Klatu esped.

A friend of Lily's, esped Ploo. *She can fix our spacecraft.*

What makes you think I cannot fix our spacecraft myself? Klatu esped.

What makes me think that? Living with you makes me think that.

I am very hurt, esped Klatu.

Where is the hide-a-craft I dropped? Ploo esped. Did you bring it?

We, uh, forgot to pick it up before we left, esped Klatu.

Well, we have to find the hide-a-craft after we look for Jo-Jo, Ploo esped. If not, we will not even know where our spacecraft _is_. Will the people who lent you this car mind if we keep it a little longer?

Lek and Klatu looked at each other.

We will send them some platinum coins, esped Klatu.

We will send them a _lot_ of platinum coins, esped Lek.

There was only one guard at the main gate. He walked away to have a smoke. Ploo, Lek, and Klatu crept to the car and sneaked inside.

Okay, Klath, Lek esped. Let us go!

But there was one problem. Klatu's legs no longer reached the floor. Before, he had been human size. Now he was too short.

Klatu, you turn the wheel, esped Lek. *I will lie on the floor and push the pedals. Hmm. Which pedal makes it stop and which one makes it go?*

Klatu told him. Then he turned the key. The engine started up with a loud roar.

The guard stared openmouthed. A car with no driver and no lights whipped around in front of him. Then, tires squealing and kicking up clouds of dust, it roared away into the desert.

Turn the page for a passage from
the second exciting book in
the weird planet series!

Huge posters on the walls showed JoJo the tiger doing circus tricks. Standing on her hind legs. Jumping through a hoop of fire. Posing with Sigmund and Rolf, the famous Las Vegas magicians.

The woman in charge of JoJo's cage wore a sparkly white jumpsuit. She was standing off to the side of the room, talking on her cell phone.

The small human girl standing next to the cage squealed with happiness. "Tigger!" she said. She reached through the bars of the cage to pet JoJo, but her arm wasn't long enough. "Pet Tigger!" she said.

She stuck her shoulder through the bars and reached out again. Her arm still wasn't long enough to reach the tiger. She squeezed between the bars and into the tiger's cage.

The woman in the sparkly white

jumpsuit didn't see this. She was too busy talking on her phone. She wandered out of the room.

Ploo was shocked to see what the little human girl had done. She ran up to the tiger's cage.

Ploo, what are you doing? Lek esped.

Going into the cage to save the little human, Ploo esped.

Do not do that! Lek esped. The stripy thing will eat you!

Ploo squeezed between the bars of the tiger's cage. She grabbed the little girl and tried to push her back through the bars.

"No!" said the little girl, struggling. "Tigger! Pet Tigger!" She refused to let Ploo push her out of the cage.

Ploo, watch out! esped Lek. The stripy thing is coming!

Ploo turned around. Uh-oh! The stripy

thing was padding heavily over to Ploo and the little girl. It looked a lot bigger and scarier now that she was inside the cage. Then Ploo had an idea:

I will morph into an animal with a long trunk and huge ears. Stripy things are afraid of animals with long trunks and huge ears. I read that in Earth Animal Studies.

It is too dangerous to morph into something that much bigger than you are! Lek warned.

You cannot morph from one shape to another! esped Klatu. Not unless you wait one arp! Not unless you go back to your true shape first!

Do not worry! Ploo esped. I have done this dozens of times before!

Ploo tried to morph—1 . . . 2 . . . 3 . . . but nothing happened . . . 4 . . . 5 . . . 6 . . . still nothing . . . 7 . . . 8 . . . 9 . . . Her skin seemed tighter, but that was all. She still looked like a little human girl. Not like a big animal with a trunk, tusks, and huge ears.

The, uh, morphing does not seem to be going so well, Ploo esped.

I told you not to do this! esped Lek. Did I tell you not to do this?

The tiger began to growl.

Morph, Ploo, morph! Lek esped.

Please morph, Ploo! Klatu esped.

Judith Greenburg

About the Author

Dan Greenburg has written everything from books and magazine articles to advertisements, plays, and movie scripts. But his favorite work is writing for kids, and he's had otherworldly success with popular series such as The Zack Files. Dan lives with his wife, author J. C. Greenburg, and his son, Zack, in a house on the Hudson River, which they share with several cats.